MASKED INNOCENCE

SAWYER QUINN

CONTENTS

Masked Innocence – Sawyer Quinn

© 2022 Sawyer Quinn

Cover by: Victoria Ivy

Victoria

The kitty to my cat.

The meow to my purr.

The saucer to my milk.

May we forever tear each other to shreds.

1

Genius or madness possessed Lady Katherine Mandeville, and only time would tell which of the two dominated her evening. Madness, she had little doubt.

Even the most brazen of women wouldn't be seen in nothing but a shift, but Kitty arrived at Halcyon House in so much less. No petticoats, no skirts. Nothing but elaborate paint to mimic an Egyptian queen beneath a black satin mask. A corset and delicate cream silk, draped from naked shoulder to bare toes, were the only things shielding her from the lurid gazes of the intimate gathering.

There was no telling where Georgiana procured the Grecian gown, and Kitty tried to imagine George at such a party. It was entirely possible, she'd been the one to tempt Kitty to attend, but she couldn't reconcile George having attended without sharing every sordid detail. Details she'd soon be party to, because it was too late for modesty and privilege. She'd already embarked on her illicit venture into feathers, candles, and immorality, and there was no turning back.

The prying eyes of each guest threatened to expose her for the fraud she was, vowing her destruction if she gave half a reason.

Dozens.

Hundreds, perhaps.

They littered every available surface, naked as the ivory statues on display, sparking an interesting sensation low in her belly. Kitty clung to the wall, praying she'd go unrecognized, and she had, so far.

In the past half hour, she'd seen more, heard more, than she ever could have conjured in her own imagination. Not even a best friend's lewd stories about the dissolute side of society prepared Kitty for the sensations consuming her.

As much as she'd like to blame Georgiana, it was her own hunger that brought her to Tristan's celebration of hedonism. The allure of the forbidden, the promise of a first kiss, had her agreeing before she could think.

Now she faced the ramifications of that choice, temptation and lust so much stronger than reckless anticipation. Every corner of the lavishly decorated drawing room overflowed with scandalous displays of human nature against a backdrop of ancient Greece. Scenes she never could have conceived if she hadn't witnessed them with her own chaste eyes, and acts so debased and dirty she was ruined before she'd ever been touched.

Somehow, it didn't detract from the splendor of golden satin draped over windows, and tables piled high with fruits and champagne. Lewd acts enhanced the ethereal scene, candles casting couples in light and shadow, illuminating and hiding in a tantalizing display.

She would never be the same after that moment. Perhaps even her mother would notice the dark mark staining her soul.

If she had any sense, she'd leave that instant, but sense abandoned her before she ever crossed the threshold, ravenousness in her need to take in every detail. George's brother was well known for his parties, but she never envisioned anything close to what he'd prepared for the evening.

Scented oils kept a musky, floral, and quite seductive enchantment over the intimate space. A sultry compliment to the moans enticing her further down the path of damnation. Moans of pain, of pleasure, of every emotion in between. Coaxed to life with both savage strikes, and tender touch.

And those sneaking off to find seclusion in rooms above had Kitty's imagination running rampant. Stolen away by a handsome, titled, gentleman would be quite an adventure.

Her sandals rooted to the floor, her inquisitive mind so far off the arranged path she'd never arrive home the same prudish debutante she'd been while sneaking away from her cloister.

She could never be that girl again.

That sensation in her belly turned to fire, growing with each passing moment, every scene that should have repulsed, beckoned instead. Her breaths came harder as a swarm of bees hummed and tumbled through her stomach, demanding she seek out more titillation.

Fan the flames into a raging fire she desired beyond reason.

A kiss would be the least of her experiences that evening if she succumbed. One would lead to another, and then another, until wild abandon made her indiscernible from every other woman in that room. A prospect she hadn't bargained for but became more difficult to resist with each passing moment.

Kitty didn't recognize the woman possessing her body, but the insistent urges weren't going to push her away from that wall, or tempt her to join the blatant acts in the open room. The bees were loud, nauseating, the string quartet suddenly too loud over the sensual sounds of pleasure.

Pleasure she wanted, but couldn't access.

Half a breath from abandoning her plans, a voice smoother than brandy, and just as decadent, fanned her ear and sent all that fire raging through her veins until it claimed every last bit of her body. "You look as though you need this."

Before she could turn, a much needed glass of champagne was pressed into her palm, and a tantalizingly dark presence invaded the tiny space she'd claimed.

Hair blacker than a sinner's soul was cropped short, just barely curling over his ears, and framing fathomless green eyes. Broad shoulders branched out from either side of his linen tunic, and her eyes refused to let the sight go.

Nothing prohibited her from perusing the Godlike physique in the flesh, far warmer, more inviting, than its cold marble counterparts. Marc Antony to her Cleopatra.

He wore no elaborate face mask to hide his identity, a bold move. Arrogant. She expected nothing less from a man renowned for his conspicuous absence from polite society and frequent attendance at gaming hells and brothels.

A rake in the truest sense.

The Marquess of Claireborne.

And he had her cornered, petrified, *wanton*.

"You've no idea how much I need it."

"I offer something far more flavorful than champagne." The way he traced the gossamer silk with starving eyes, like he hadn't seen a meal in days, seduced her body and mind and left her dripping from her most forbidden passages. "I can soothe away your hesitations, bring you rapture in their stead."

She'd served herself up on a silver platter, to him and every other male in attendance, and she could certainly do much worse than the marquess.

If they were discovered, there would be an entire issue of *On Dit* dedicated to her decadent and salacious fall from grace. No respectable man would touch her, and her father would see her packed off before dawn broke. But the whispered promise fanned across her cheek as he closed the last of the respectable distance between them, and all those little bees dissipated.

"Curious?" He ran his thumb down the back of her arm, setting an instant flutter loose in her belly, tempting her with its illicit promise.

Curious was hardly the word she'd use. Scandalized. Fascinated. Deprived.

Aroused.

She scanned the room, draining the glass as her cheeks burned. The open display of naked bodies, the sensual confidence engulfing the room, created an ache for something she couldn't name, for things she didn't understand. Intimate things that sent liquid fire to places that'd never been warm before.

But *he* could show her.

A serpent to her Eve, offering fruit so forbidden she'd leave that party ruined beyond repair. All it took was one tiny taste, and she'd trade the burden of innocence for one of illicit knowledge.

"As a kitten." Kitty swallowed down the last of her hesitation, as the marquess snaked his arm around her waist, glittering eyes betraying every sordid thought in his mind.

His touch made everything real.

Undeniably real.

With an easy elegance, he shifted to block her view. The room, the smells, the people, all melted away as he commanded her attention. "Don't worry about them. Make tonight about you, little flower. The insatiable curiosity that rivals my own."

Every debased act she'd witnessed taunted her, promised everything she'd gone there in search of, and so much more. A tingle ran up her spine, quickening her heart and constricting her chest. "And what is it, exactly, you're curious about?"

He smiled, so full of vicious promise as he tipped her chin up, forcing her gaze to his. "You."

2

It was a rare flower Sebastian discovered amongst the weeds, and every moment in her presence sent his heart beating faster.

The apprehension pouring from such an exquisite blossom lured him closer, teased an experience far beyond what he'd anticipated. Such a specimen of feminine perfection belonged nowhere but his bed.

The silk seductively draping her shoulders did far less to conceal her than the mask hiding her face. Delectable curves flared from a trim waist, and her full breasts threatened to burst from the low-cut gown. With her kohl rimmed eyes and onyx mask, she left him ravenous for a meal he hadn't enjoyed in some time.

With a gentle hand to the small of her back, he guided her toward the marbled stairs rising to the bedrooms above. "And how is it such a rare and beautiful thing found her way here?"

"I've never done anything like this." As he opened the door and ushered her into the dimly lit room, a shiver ran through her. Eyes darting to the bed, never shifting, and a hard swallow betrayed the nervousness thrumming through her body. "A close friend secured an invitation, and the temptation was too much to resist."

The lock clicked, deafening in the ominous silence, and a whimper so sweet and delectable brushed past her lips. "That much, you've already made obvious, little flower. I count myself fortunate I was the one to pluck you from the weeds."

He'd commit every moment and detail of their interlude to memory. The sultry voice, her gold and green flecked eyes, and the intoxicating scent of violet clinging to her skin. A scent harkening to his own innocence, spring in Yorkshire heralding their impending departure to London so his mother could enjoy the last few months of the season.

A circus he disliked as a boy and loathed as a man.

Finally tearing her eyes from the bed, she met his gaze again. Short rapid breaths shifted her bare shoulders, drawing attention to the pristine flesh. "There's something I should tell you." A flush in her cheeks peeked from beneath the mask, though it was difficult to determine if it was anticipation or fear coaxing the color.

The flickering light of a lone candle danced over her skin, casting an ethereal glow. A fallen angel who'd landed in his bed, imploring him to show her the darkest side of sin. The sweet flower in his grasp was certainly unlike any other, and it was only fitting she possessed a distinctive fragrance so evocative.

"Your body, the responsiveness already so evident, will tell me anything I need to know." He ran his fingers over her exposed collarbone, coaxing a soft sigh from supple lips as her eyes slipped closed.

Parted lips he ached to caress with his own, to plumb their depths and discover if she tasted as sweet as her floral scent, if the innocence in her demeanor echoed in her kiss. How deeply her manicured nails would rake down his back as he plundered her sweet depths.

If he allowed her hands freedom.

The allure of trussing her up for his uninhibited pleasure edged his control to slipping. The evening was young, and so was she, leaving ample time for indulgences, and he swiped his finger across her lower lip, envisioning its plump softness cradling the head of his cock.

The beast stirred, preparing to bring every last one of her fantasies to life. "Have you ever pleasured a man with your mouth?"

She took a lip, red as climbing roses, between pearly teeth as her timid gaze dipped to his pelvis, and he allowed her to take her fill uninterrupted. As she slowly dragged her gaze up, the tip of her tongue slipped out to slicken her bottom lip. "No."

A single word embodying a dangerous curiosity, her unabashed innocence a refreshing change from the experienced whores and actresses who frequented his bed. He'd be her second, maybe third, and the evidence of her first time being so botched stared up at him from beneath thick black lashes.

There would be no well-practiced seduction from her that evening, and it would be worth every scrap of genuine coyness he received in exchange. Every first he'd gift her with. Every other time would be banished from her memory, and the timid girl before him would blossom into the lustful creature hiding beneath her fear.

There was no sweeter fruit than a ripened cherry begging to be tasted, and her pleasure would bring on his own rapture.

"I'm afraid you'll find me painfully inexperienced." She stepped closer to the fire, running her hands over her upper arms. Whether it was the cold or her trepidation driving her there, it hardly mattered; he'd soothe both before the night was through.

"We're going to go slow tonight, little flower." Sebastian slipped behind her, pressing his lips to a shoulder, drinking in the intoxicating scent. Another shiver ran through her, and she offered her sleek neck to his eager mouth.

Trailing kisses along the curved path, he traced his thumbs over her exposed back, drifting lower until they found the row of buttons keeping her from his view. One by one they slipped free, the white silk parting slowly to bare the rest of her succulent flesh. "And your journey down the Nile this evening *will* be a memorable one."

Curious as a little cat, she peeked over her shoulder, that seductive bottom lip caught between her teeth again, as if she knew exactly what she was doing. Temptation to take it between his own warred against his self-control, so eager for a bite.

"There isn't a drop of dew upon your petals that will go untasted by morning." He scraped his teeth along her neck as he slipped the silk from her shoulder, allowing it to fall in a puddle at her feet. Patience was his ally; too much, too quickly, and she could wilt into the wallflower she'd been when he plucked her from the garden of sin.

A wallflower with the potential to flee if not handled properly.

What he needed beyond reason was an unhindered view of her face, but events at Halcyon House were met with strict rules requiring Sebastian get explicit permission. "The mask. Shall we take it off?"

"I'm willing to indulge in a lot of things this evening, but sacrificing anonymity is not one of them." The adamancy, the fire blazing in those hazel eyes, demanded his acceptance. The only women who hid were those keeping secrets, and the intrigue of hers was too much to ignore. "The ramifications of my being here far surpass yours, so you'll forgive my lack of eagerness to satisfy your curiosity."

Bone deep need to unveil her secrets combated warning bells sounding at her dire admission. There were scant few who would attend that gathering while fretting a ruined reputation. A rational man would hesitate at the very least, consider the meaning of those ramifications, but rationality stood no chance against the siren before him.

Offering herself to a man so impatient to have her had his cock throbbing more painfully with each passing moment. Luring him to a death he'd welcome gladly so long as he'd satisfied them both before it came.

Delicately, he released the strings of the corset, each moment taken with absolute care, until it was just another bit of fabric at her magnificent feet. It would take longer than one night to worship the goddess he'd pulled from the stars.

He raked his gaze from the crown of her blonde curls to the tips of her bare toes as he made a slow circle, and when he caught the inquisitive look in her expressive eyes, he nearly lost control. Curious, yet timid as a dove. Creamy and statuesque, as if carved from marble by the most skilled craftsmen, and unveiled before him.

Only him.

Every drop of blood in his veins pumped to his cock, as he absorbed each tantalizing bit of her flesh. Timid. Curious. Bold. There was so much of her for him to digest as she met his stare, taking meager attempts to shield her nakedness. One arm crossed over her breasts as the other shielded her cunt, her breaths coming quicker, fueling the lust raging through his body.

There was little he could do against it. "You are, without a doubt, the most delectable creature I will ever have the pleasure of plunging headfirst into."

The anxious glint in her eyes lured his lust closer to the surface, and it seeped from every pore like an aphrodisiac. "My Lord, I *really* must confess something."

He touched his finger to her lips to quiet her words. "There are no titles in this room, little flower. Take a breath, and rest assured every desire will be fulfilled tonight."

"How could you possibly know what my desires are?" She ran cautious fingers along his arm, sending shivers of anticipation through every nerve ending as she abandoned modesty for curiosity. "We don't even know one another."

"I don't need to know who you are to know what pleases a woman as delicate as you." He motioned his chin over her shoulder and crept in closer, until her taut nipples brushed against his chest. "Get on the bed."

Each hesitant backward step toward the mattress was met with a sure footed one of his own, until the four posters, with their draping burgundy brocade canopy, became an arching backdrop to her defilement. With each step, she took in a dragging breath. The sight of her bared breasts, tipped with peony pink, leaving him starved for air.

He reached for the lengths of rope on the nightstand, grateful for Tristan's unfailing attention to detail. When her legs hit the bed, she pushed herself back, each one taking its turn to tempt him as she crept farther from his grasp. Frightened anticipation dripped from her as she pressed her thighs tightly together, eyes fixed on the fibrous braid.

Every movement, every delicate line of her body, called to him as she settled in the middle of the bed, resting on her arms, and locking her hazel eyes with his. A dare for him to abandon reason and forsake leisurely exploration. "Grip your ankles."

The obedient little thing did exactly as she was told, each of her shuddered breaths betraying the lust coursing through her own veins.

Despite her apprehension, she boldly offered herself completely for his pleasure, and his heart pulsed in his throat. It'd been months since he last indulged in a woman, and breaking his celibacy with such a sweet blossom was far more than he deserved.

Slowly, so temptingly, she traced her fingers lightly down her thighs. Over the sweet arches of her knees. Caressed her calves. All in a torturous display of obedience, and he felt her flesh as surely as it'd been his own fingers trailing that path.

He bound her wrists to her ankles, exposing all of her, allowing him unhindered access to her most delectable parts. Like a beacon in a storm, that most sacred place between her legs beckoned him, arousal glistening in the dim light and inviting him to have a taste.

"Wet and wanting." He flicked his eyes up to hers, a half smile crossing his lips as he forced the last of his restraint. "Absolute perfection."

Her brow furrowed slightly, but she didn't say a word or shift away. Rather, she met his gaze as more gooseflesh broke out over her skin. The room was cool, the fire no match for the brutally cold winter. But even the frost coating the windows did nothing to calm his randy cock in its bid to burst free of its buckskin restraint.

With care, he accepted the welcoming call of the delicate petal settled upon a featherbed and stalked the primal space between each bound ankle. First, one knee, his knuckles, their eyes never wavering until he pressed his lips to her inner thigh and took a slow, deliberate breath.

A sharp gasp crossed her lips, and he gripped around her thigh, kissing the opposite and drawing a low moan as she arched into the bed. The shakiness in her breaths as she shifted restlessly encouraged him to taste her. Bring her off in a way she'd not soon forget.

He slipped his fingers between her folds, gently parting and baring every last spot to his ravenous gaze. The first time he ran his finger over her, she jerked against the ropes binding her as a gasped cry escaped her lips. Her hips arched off the bed, feeding his need for her complete submission and release.

"Bound. Naked. Desperate." He let out a moan, and a whimper crossed her lips as he gave in to temptation, running his tongue over dewy flesh. Each frustrated tug at her restraints, the accompanying cry, resonated through him. A firm grip on her hips kept her close to him, exactly where he'd provide the sweetest torment, until he was ready to allow her release.

With each swipe of his tongue, she struggled harder, to get away or draw closer, and the thrill of the fight fed them both. A tormented moan crossed her lips, and he chuckled against her skin, placing a soft kiss to each inner thigh. "Could you be more exquisite?"

A savory sweetness sat on the tip of his tongue, and her musky arousal urged him to steal every drop of her essence as a reward for his valiant efforts to stay his cock. Never had he indulged in anything so wickedly delectable, and it drove a need to mark her as indelibly as she'd marked him.

With each moan, she pressed harder against his tongue, pleaded for rapture, and each time he thought her on the brink, he backed off. Slipping his overeager tongue over less intensely affected regions of her cunt, reveling in her cries of anguish each time.

"You're teasing me." Her toes curled into the mattress, fingertips frantically seeking purchase, but with no give to her bonds every effort was futile.

"*You* tease *me* with every graceful quiver of your thighs and mewling cry for release." His cock strained against his breeches, demanding freedom and satisfaction, but he had so much more to show the lotus blossom before he claimed her for his own. "Teasing leads to the greatest ecstasy."

He kissed the soft, wet flesh between her thighs, and smiled when her brows stitched together over her nose, her fight against the restraints growing more frenzied.

With so much more pleasure to be had, it would be a shame if the flower bloomed before she was ready.

3

The moment the Marquess picked up the unforgiving jute, she should have protested, but fascination and wonder compelled her to continue pushing her boundaries.

Being at his mercy. The care he took to elicit pleasure. The inability to do anything but accept his carnal intent. It all swirled and surged through her, hot and cold, and overwhelming with the need for something unknown. Every brush of his skin rippled outward, the heat of his breath against her core pooling in her pelvis, uncovering a well she hadn't known existed until he filled it.

There was something so deliciously wicked in his eyes when he looked up at her from between thighs she never imagined would be parted by the Marquess of Claireborne. Each forbidden touch dragged her further into the depths of depravity he was already so comfortable in.

If that was wicked, she never wanted to be virtuous again.

As his lips reached that most intimate part of her, anticipation left her quivering and weak beneath him. Once more, his finger slid easily between her legs, trailing over the sensitive nub, sending a jolt through her spine. And his tongue.

Oh God, his tongue.

It continued its lazy exploration, delving inside and lapping up between her folds. His sinful caresses held the key to something so barbaric and dark she'd never recover.

She convulsed beneath him as he circled languidly over the nub he'd just teased, every gentle flick sending waves of pleasure to match the movement of her hips. They moved in pace, her body possessing a mind of its own, and the wanton moans coming from her own mouth added a new layer of embarrassment. So similar to the cries she'd been terrified of downstairs, and he'd commanded them from her without ever saying a word.

In the midst of their slow, rolling, waves, his mouth closed over her for the first time. Wet heat dripped from her bottom as she lifted off the bed, and a low, guttural moan filled the dark room and vibrated through her. Pleasure and passion surrounded every centimeter of flesh, wrapped around her throat, and dragged her into an abyss without escape.

Without desire for escape.

She'd been liberated from the bonds of duty, honor, and reputation by a rake with his lips suckled around her, and he'd yet to even ruin her properly.

Muscled arms curled around dainty thighs, exposing her completely to his fiendish lips and tongue, forcing her open for his assault. Licking and sucking until torment and pleasure tangled into a web of need. She could do nothing but lay back and accept the sweet offering, crying out when it became too much to bear.

Every one of her cries renewed his efforts. Drove his tongue deeper into her, carrying her from the depths of immorality to the highest peaks of hedonism. His single-minded pursuit ripped sanity away and left her helplessly writhing beneath him.

He dragged his teeth over the bundle of nerves, biting gently and eliciting a low groan from her as she struggled against the restraints. There was something just out of reach, a pinnacle she was compelled to climb, and she was so close.

Her cries came closer, sharper, hips bucking against his mouth, seeking more friction. Releasing her thighs, he fisted the ropes binding her and tugged them hard, pinning her to the mattress and his mouth, preventing any meaningful movement and leaving her entirely at his complete lack of mercy.

With an expert flick of his tongue, he sucked her between his lips and launched her over that edge, senses exploding, overwhelming rational thought.

The chill in the air, and the heat of his mouth. Sweat coated her skin, and the demonic possession of her body as she convulsed beneath him dug the ropes deeper into her sensitive flesh. The soft downy mattress beneath her, the silk sheets clutched in her fingers, the scruff of his cheeks scraping her thighs as she clamped them tight around his head, the only things keeping her tethered to sanity.

As the assault slowly receded, she fluttered back down to him.

He continued licking at her, slowly and delicately, as she floated back to earth. Back to the brocade curtains in the candlelight, the dim room and garnet cloak from society. An apt metaphor for the depths of hell she'd most certainly reside in after what they'd done.

Loosening her grip on the black silk beneath her, ragged breaths calmed to deep inhales and slow exhales. Every languid swipe of his tongue sent renewed shockwaves, though nothing as shattering as the climax she'd reached.

Candlelight cast flickering shadows against the heavy fabric and his shoulders, muscles shifting in the glow. He lifted his head, swiping the back of his hand over his mouth with a smirk.

Half his face shone in the moonlight sneaking into paradise, emerald eyes heavy on her body and unwavering in their intensity as he released her bonds. Each limb was massaged in turn, a gentle kiss bestowed on each before he laid them down.

Dragging his lips up her body, he twined his fingers with hers and lifted them over her head, pinning them to the mattress. The embers in her core fanned back to life, as the arrogant rake made good on his promise. Giving her so much more than knowledge and solidifying his place in her memory.

"Can you show me more?"

His chuckle brushed over her cheek as he nudged the edge of her mask with his nose. "So much more, my flower. You're the most delicious bud I've ever had the pleasure of tasting, and I don't plan on letting you go. Not until we're both sated and panting"

Burying his face into her neck, he bit gently, sucking, and soothing with his tongue.

His pelvis pressed into hers, a rock-hard bulge rocking into her, offering friction she was desperate for all over again. A longing to explore his body as he did hers was overwhelming, but she was just as helpless with her wrists in his hands as when they were bound to her ankles.

"I don't," she took a slow breath, exhaling on a soft moan as he tilted his hips, pressing harder into her. "I don't know."

"Let's see how ready you are for me." He released one of her wrists, then trailed an overeager finger down her arm, over her breast, across her belly, and lower. Thrusting against her again brought a gasp to fill the space between them. "Because I am *so* ready for you, my little blossom."

He slipped a finger into her entrance, stretching and burning as she was breached for the first time. But he'd barely penetrated when he stopped abruptly.

Confusion passed over his features, chased quickly by disbelief. He sat up, going back on his heels as his eyes met hers, accusatory even in the dim light. The truth was in the open, the confession he'd refused to hear from her lips expressed plainly in a way he couldn't silence or deny.

Fear he'd refuse to continue choked her, and she licked her lips nervously, unwilling to look away. There was nothing she could do or say as every conceivable emotion took its turn commanding his expression.

Wonder and intrigue widened his eyes, and his breathing grew heavier in the damning silence as he shifted his gaze down between her legs. After several tense seconds, he looked back up, forehead drawn down tight, jaw clenched tight as fury took control.

"How the bloody hell did a virgin get into this party?"

4

He stared her down, heart hammering, as the full ramifications of his discovery came crashing down around them. It should have squashed his desire, dampened the fire raging inside to take what she so freely offered, instead it only spurred him on.

The lotus blossom was begging to have her petals defiled, and he struggled to remember why he must deny them both.

Availing himself of an opera girl could be forgiven, enjoying the delights offered at a brothel were all but expected. Even bedding a young widow could be reconciled. But to relieve an upper class maiden of her virginity was unforgivable.

A mark on his honor that could never be removed.

There was no question about her reputation, he'd ruined her as surely as he'd brought her to her first *petite mort.* That didn't mean he need join her on further exploits to satisfy her carnal curiosity. As she stared up at him with wide terrified eyes, a single question echoed in his brain, demanding answers. "Who are you?"

"No one of consequence." She shook her head, voice quaking, mirroring the tremble shivering through her.

A brow raised as he huffed a humorless laugh. If she was *no one of consequence,* he was a vicar. The precipice he teetered on grew more precarious by the moment, the desire to walk away nothing compared with an unrelenting need to claim her. "Then why the mask?"

When she gave no answer, he scrubbed a hand over his face. Never had he thought himself a man of questionable integrity, but there he was facing the moral dilemma of his life. Balking at the obvious decision. The man he'd been an hour ago would rip the satin from her face, send her home, and they'd never speak of it again.

The man he'd become in that hour was somewhat less willing to end the evening so prematurely. He raked his gaze over her, mind spinning circles as he argued between what was right and what was easy. The longer he considered, the further from respectability he fell. It wasn't about wanting her, it was about *needing* her, and the indisputable fact she was untouched only heightened that need.

She'd be his. Only his. In every meaningful way, *his*.

A prospect hardening his cock rather than calming it.

"Take. Off. The. Mask." Each word was bit off, forced through clenched teeth as he demanded her identity. To take full stock of his choice before damning himself to hell. It wasn't shyness driving her to maintain anonymity, it was their now mutual knowledge her virginity was worth more than any dowry she may possess.

"No." Not once did her eyes waver from his, not even for a moment, but the response was a mere whisper between them.

The word scarcely crossed her lips when he gripped her wrists, pinning them to the mattress above her head once more. His lips crushed hers, his tongue forcing its way into her mouth when a surprised gasp gave it a chance. A punishing kiss, controlled, aggressive, and full of frightening intent. Because he'd made his choice, and he could only pray hers would save them both.

Damning himself to hell was one thing, burdening her with a lifetime of condemnation for a few moments of bliss was quite another. With her virtue still physically intact, no one would ever have to know what they'd done.

What *he'd* done.

Rather than pull away, she met his passion with her own. The initial shock giving way to the curiosity cursing them both. With tentative strokes, her own tongue met his, and her lithe body shifted against him, hips rolling in a sensual dance they had no right partaking in. She kissed him as deeply as he did her, matching aggression with aggression, driving him further out of his mind.

When a soft moan slipped from her mouth to his, he abruptly released her and pushed up, both panting as they stared across the chasm between them. "I don't know what compelled you here tonight, but you're damned lucky I found you."

There were so many other men there. Men with inclinations toward violence, who would relish the thought of a virgin without a care or consideration for her pleasure. Or consent.

The thought of her ending up at their hands left a pit in his stomach that threatened to swallow him whole. The fertile bloom before him came in search of knowledge and experience, something he could provide her. He could provide that, and so much more.

Safety. Pleasure. Protection.

But *she* needed to be sure.

"You're still unspoiled, darling. Untainted. If we stop now, no one ever has to know." He traced her bottom lip with his thumb, tugging it from between her teeth, the urge to take it between his own once more threatening his already precarious grip on sanity. "If we continue, you'll be ruined in the most literal sense."

"I want to know everything. Experience everything." The earnest plea stoked his desire to damn himself to eternal hell and take what wasn't his. Her tongue darted out and swiped across that plump bottom lip, leaving it glistening and pleading to be captured between his teeth.

But he had no right to take her lips with his, to bite or tease. No right to imagine those decadent lips wrapped around the swollen head of his cock. She was an innocent, and already he'd been her guide down the path of true wickedness.

Before his eyes, the fear gave way to resolve, and she reached up for him. Breaths faster and harder as her fingertips delicately brushed over his arms. Flicking her eyes between his face and where her fingers brushed his skin, a boldness overtook her, and her feathered touch turned confident, exploring the lines and hollows of muscle.

A curious little kitten who played dirty in a game she had no business engaging in. Every bit of her had been brought into the dim candlelight, his mouth had explored her most sacred recesses, but still she refused to reveal her face.

There were so few women who would give themselves so completely while maintaining their anonymity so ardently. Such a woman, by all logic, never would have darkened Tristan's doorstep. Wouldn't have even known of the party. And yet, there she was. Virginal and young.

Which meant only one damning thing.

"Tell me who you are." He pushed off the bed, morality making one last stand.

A defiant shake of her head as she followed him up, grazing her nose against his chest. Tentative fingers slipped around him and over his back as she inhaled, the newfound confidence surging straight to his cock.

"No." Slowly, she went up on her knees and traced a featherlight touch up the side of his neck, until her nails raked through his hair and sent chills down to his heels. She was convincing, with those hazel eyes locked with his, a hard, desperate swallow the only betrayal to any lingering unease.

"Your virtue is worth something. To your future groom, your mama." Him, mostly. His cock, not at all. The bloody fucker was rooting for her hymen to be obliterated. That bottom lip pulled back between her teeth, and as he reached to tug it free a groan escaped his own lips.

Morality didn't stand a chance.

"If I was concerned about a future husband, I never would have stepped foot into Halcyon House in the first place, let alone climbed those stairs at your side." A small smile played on her lips as she tugged his hair until he exposed his neck, her lips seeking him as his had sought her. "And my mama died a long time ago."

They were both yearning to forsake everything they valued, and for no reason other than his heart was wanting and his cock was eager. She was just as sensual, just as eager, to plunge as far into the obsidian abyss as he. Her innocence was for want of opportunity, not a lack of willingness.

He disentangled her arms from his neck and stepped back, standing before her and staring down from his full height. A hard exhale left her when he tugged the tunic over his head, and he let her take her time. Eyes wandering from shoulders to waist and back. When she lifted her glassy eyes to his, luscious lips parted, he found a hunger rivaling his own.

If she wanted ruin, he'd gladly lay waste to every sacred part of her body.

5

Her imagination hadn't come close to reality, and a chest that put Greek gods to shame stole the breath from her lungs. Hard planes and shadowed grooves defined every muscle, the candlelight driving her eyes to every exposed piece of flesh.

She burned to trace the sprinkling of hair on his lower belly into his breeches, and then farther.

A significant bulge at the base of the trail caught her eye, and she couldn't shift them away. The little knowledge she possessed told her that what lay beneath the soft fabric would relieve her of her virginity. Unfortunately, that knowledge didn't extend far enough to tell her exactly how it was supposed to manage the job.

The space his fingers barely breached was far too small to accommodate what he hid beneath the buckskin. She'd scarcely accommodated his finger.

That was ever so much larger.

Moments ago, it was pressed against her, teased her with possibilities of unholy pleasure and roguish debauchery. She thought she'd seen enough downstairs to have an idea of what lay in wait for her, but the reality was far more frightening up close, and exceedingly personal. Fear and exhilaration fought for control as she edged ever closer to discovery.

Shifting on her knees, Kitty crept closer, eyes locked on the bulge she was so hungry to uncover. There'd been a multitude of reasons she attended that masquerade, and one of them was standing right in front of her.

Tall, broad, dangerous to her sensibilities, and gave her body a safe haven to explore her sinful cravings. *That* was what she came for, and uncertainty slipped away, leaving only brazen desire and a need to discover every last part of him.

He caught her chin with the crook of his finger, green eyes searching for something he'd have a very difficult time finding. "Are you certain?"

"With every corrupted bit of my body."

Without a second more of hesitation, he shoved his breeches to the floor, allowing the monster beneath the bulge to spring from its confines. The appendage was thicker than even her vivid imagination prepared her for.

It commanded attention, the round tip jutting toward her from between powerful thighs. She bit down on her lower lip, eager to taste him, enjoy him, as he'd enjoyed her. Relished tasting and nibbling at her most private and forbidden parts. An act so wickedly sinful, and so incredibly satisfying for them both.

Desire to experience the same satisfaction drove her to reach out. Only, she hesitated just before touching the ferocious beast, and took a slow, brave look up to shadowed eyes.

He gave a tight nod as his hands fisted at his sides, and she brushed her fingers lightly over the velvet skin sheathing thick steel.

Clear fluid oozed from the tip, and her tongue swiped across her lips involuntarily, as her hand drew back. The drop glistened in the candlelight and lured her attention like a moth to a flame.

Collecting the pearly drop on the pad of his thumb, he offered it up to her. Attention bouncing from luscious drop to scorching eyes, she parted her lips in acquiescence. With her breath calm and her body pulsing, Kitty slipped her lips around him. Savoring, memorizing, the moment and the taste of him on her tongue.

She closed her eyes as the marquess gently pulled his thumb from her mouth, scraping it against her teeth, and she whimpered as the drop melted away to nothing but a memory. A memory that would torment with promises of what could be.

An agonized groan rumbled in his chest as he slipped his moist thumb down her chin, before it was gone. "Bloody hell."

A look down revealed another drop where the first had been. A bit larger. Demanding it not be wasted. With a swipe of her thumb, she scooped it up and slipped it into her mouth as a shiver ran up the marquess' imposing body. That shiver had her mouth dripping, and the nub between her thighs throbbing.

Painfully.

"When you asked about pleasuring a man with my mouth, had you meant taking *you* into my mouth as you did me?" The words fumbled as she glanced to his loins and back up, but the lust seeping from his eyes stayed her thrashing heart as surely as she'd been bound. Though her heart was hammering, and curiosity surged her forward, inexperience held her by the reins.

"That would be *exactly* what I meant." He brushed his knuckles over her mask and down her cheek, triggering a tingling sensation over her skin that could only be remedied by the marquess himself.

The prospect of slipping her lips around his tip, filling her mouth completely, had her shifting to edge off the aching need building between her thighs. "Shall I?"

"No, little flower." He shook his head and leaned a knee on the edge of the bed, dipping it beneath his weight as he hunted her down. Adrenaline surged her heart, and tightened her stomach, as she edged backward. "Right now, I want to show you how it's meant to be."

She reclined into the plush down as his eyes and hands roved her body, the unexpected soft calluses abraded her skin and burned in a new memory to keep her company at night. There was a new wildness in his eyes, and rather than Eve in the garden, Kitty was a fox caught in the hunt.

Whatever was about to happen outweighed everything that'd come before, and her heart vaulted into her throat as she slid back. It was a tipping point. A precipice she'd been entirely too eager to leap from.

Once the full weight of gravity settled around her, she wasn't as confident in her willingness to jump. She needed space, a moment to clear her head. A second to consider how far she was truly willing to go.

Which was already further than she'd ever intended.

Then, he straightened to his full height and fisted the base of his rigid length, leaving her laid out on the bed beneath him. Every breath he took shifted his entire body. An eternity he stood there, drinking his fill as he stroked himself. Every methodical movement melted away her fear and dampened the silk under her bottom.

The sight of his fist sliding over hardened satin, his shuddered breaths, the lust in eyes as he raked them over her, left her dizzy and heady with a power she never imagined possessing.

She was Eve once again, wanting and eager to fall from grace.

And without any regard for her station, fortune, or any other superficial reason other men showed interest in her. Even her face was still covered, leaving him nothing but her body, her reactions, to spur him on. The powerful, magnificent man above her was beside himself with lust.

For *her.*

Lord Claireborne shifted his knee, and the bed dipped lower as he came between her legs, crawling over her body and pressing her further into the mattress. Rugged determination oozed from every pore as she scraped her nails through his hair and dragged a growl from deep within his chest.

The primal sound fed her confidence and compelled her calves around his thighs, the heat of his body nothing to the raging inferno edging her toward combustion. The fires of hell enveloped her as he kissed her shoulder, her neck, all while his feral, needy sounds bored into her soul.

There was nothing but the Marquess of Claireborne, nothing but his bare thighs pressed against hers, eliminating everything but his touch and the heaviness of his presence.

She ran her hands over the taut muscles of his arms, the lines of his torso, every sliver of him she could reach. For one night, Lady Katherine Mandeville could be no one. Indulge all she wanted, taste all she wanted, and she intended to make good use of her *very* precious time.

Like before, his hand slipped between their bodies and he eased a finger inside. "This will hurt, flower, but the pain will ebb."

The question of what would hurt sat on her tongue, but he circled his finger, and an uncomfortable burn tempered the exquisite torment and stole every word. He shifted his thumb to press over that sweet spot he so expertly commanded, and she was lost to everything but him once more. The conflicting sensations coaxed from within the confines of her chaste and sheltered upbringing.

Blood thundered, and she dug her fingers deep into his shoulders as he inserted a second finger. Pain and pleasure thrashed together until the assault on her senses drifted her toward a place more and more familiar.

The burning dulled when he withdrew his hand, leaving her with an empty ache needing to be filled. Before she could manage a protest about where his fingers belonged, or who they belonged to while in that room, he gripped her chin and tilted, until she met his eyes. "I need you to be a good girl and stay relaxed for me. Even when it hurts."

A sharp nod was all she could manage, those words touching her as intimately as his fingers, sending the same warmth flooding through her. She bit her lip and took a cleansing breath, every muscle from her forehead to her toes going lax at his command.

"That's my good girl." He kissed her softly, biting her bottom lip and tugging gently as he notched at her entrance. The heat of his mouth against hers, the abrasion of his teeth raking delicate flesh, left a mark on her soul as surely as if he'd drawn blood.

A kiss she'd never forget, and so innocuous amid everything else she'd experienced in one vivid night.

There was a slight pressure in her canal as he released her from the kiss and inexorably pushed forward. The stretching was far more than it took to accommodate his fingers, but he eased in slowly and steadily. She clutched him tighter, nails digging into his rippled back, as she pressed her face against his chest.

"Deep breath, flower." The foreign invader seared through her most sensitive parts, until he thrust his way to the hilt, stilling and allowing her to acclimate, scattering soft kisses over her face. "Never have I discovered a bloom so radiant and delicate."

The reverent words gave her life, relieved some of the pain as she was assured her discomfort and inexperience didn't make her any less desirable. It took only moments for her muscles to adjust around him, the stretch giving way to delicious fullness, a feeling of rightness she couldn't comprehend.

She couldn't go the rest of her life never again feeling the way she did in that moment, with the marquess buried inside her, when everything that made her pure was stripped away. How something so good could be so wicked was beyond her comprehension.

Especially with the marquess seated so inextricably inside her.

"What's going on in that head of yours?" He pressed his lips into her neck, setting a hurricane loose in her belly as she arched back to offer him more. An invitation she needed him to accept, and one he answered with deliberate slowness as fire chased his lips across her breasts.

If they were discovered, her reputation in tatters around her, she wouldn't regret a single moment. A thousand days of persecution and exile were a fair trade for the gift Lord Claireborne had given her. "How once will never be enough."

Before another word could slip his lips, he pulled back, the sharp burn dragging a gasp as her nails plunged into his flesh. Once more he paused, giving time to adjust, for her mind to catch up.

The burning dwindled to embers, leaving the fullness she'd come to crave.

Her grip eased, and she drew her fingertips over his shoulders and up his neck, driving them through his hair. There wasn't enough of him to touch, to smell, to memorize. The silkiness of his hair amplified every sensation he'd bored into her soul, and she used her newfound power to make him feel as good as he did her. "I know there's more, I want it."

A soft groan passed his lips as he dipped his head and scattered light kisses across her shoulder as he plunged forward once more, drawing a harsh exhale as he stole her breath.

"Give it to me."

A low growl rumbled from his throat, while his thumbs dug hard into her hips, harkening to that same part of her that'd purred like a kitten as he murmured *good girl* against her skin. "Bloody hell, you're going to end me."

"And you, me."

He eased out slowly, leaving another empty space in his wake. Just before withdrawing completely, he crept forward once again. Twice he repeated the motion, and the last of her discomfort fell away, leaving a tightness and friction she craved.

On instinct, Kitty tilted her pelvis to meet his movements, the residual pain urging her on, heightening the fulfillment of every depraved fantasy drifting in her head. "Faster."

A chuckle vibrated her chest and filled the candlelit room, just before the marquess nibbled at her ear and sent a jolt through to her toes. "Are you certain?"

"Exceedingly so."

Without a second's hesitation, he set to gliding through her slick sheath, each stroke coming faster than the last. With a push off the mattress, he went to his knees, the V of his hips rolling in a tempo that sent her heart racing.

She was so lost in the motion, she'd not realized he'd grabbed her hand and brought it down between them. The implication of what he wanted her to do caught her off guard, and her eyes flew to his.

There was an intensity behind them pushing her forward, out of her comfort zone and into the depths of hell. His pelvis crashed against hers, and he fell over her, lips a hair's breadth from hers. "Pleasure yourself, as I did."

"I can't—"

"Do it." Her protest was cut off with two sharp words, and her hand flitted down until her fingertips landed over the tiny nub he'd brought back to life with little coaxing. It was slick, and the lightest touch sent a jolt radiating throughout her body. "Good girl, bring yourself off with me rooted inside you."

Drawing circles like he'd done, she carried herself closer to that zenith, where the world crashed down around her. Only this time, he was inside her, giving her even more to experience. The tightness, the fullness, the ache, the burn. It was overwhelming, and in the midst of it all she was committing the most perverted of sins. "This is wrong."

"No, little flower, it's beautiful." Sliding his hand to her thigh, he hitched her leg up, bringing him closer, deeper. The fiery fullness the single greatest gift she'd ever been given.

Each breath was met with a soft cry as her heart galloped wildly. Every part of her slick with sweat, tingling, and yearning, and out of her mind. Every vibration propelled her to the end she was eager to reach.

All at once the world around her imploded.

Clamping down tight around him, she cried her release, tugging his neck until he was buried in hers once again. His roar echoed in her ear as he gave one last powerful thrust, joining their bodies so tightly together there was a part of him she'd never lose.

A spasming low in her belly felt unusually right, some hers, some his, all of it the perfect end to a perfect act. Each of his breaths panted against her ear matched hers, everything deathly and unnaturally silent as she drifted once more from the heavens.

With a last drag of air, he went up on his elbows over her, brushing her hair away from her face. "Do not ever be ashamed of your body or what it does, little flower. It was meant for this, and there's no reason you cannot pursue your own pleasure."

She laughed weakly through her heavy breaths, his encouragement to touch herself a resolution to a problem she hadn't considered. It would have been shocking to hear from anyone else, but coming from the marquess it was as natural as every other act they'd committed that night. "Every single thing I've thought about you has been proven true tonight."

He laughed as he trailed his lips up her neck and behind her ear. "What sorts of things?"

"You, Lord Claireborne, are a man of debauchery and sin, wholly unfit for polite company." She laughed again, stronger, and clasped her hands behind his neck. "It's little wonder your mother's soiree was the only event you attended last season."

His kisses halted abruptly, and he rocked back, a single brow arched high as his eyes turned dark. "And how would you know that?"

6

I ce cascaded through his veins as the realization she was another of the *ton* hit him full force in the chest. He'd suspected, but confirmation set anger flooding, clearing the ice and making way for red hot fury as he pulled out of her. "Who are you?"

She sat up, sliding backward on the bed as she pulled the sheet to her breasts. All signs of the confident woman taking charge of her sexuality vanished, leaving behind the frightened kitten who'd lured him in. "I told you, no one."

"A bit late for modesty." As he stood, the terror in her eyes increased tenfold, and she scrambled off the bed and away from him, sheet clutched tight as she cowered behind it. "You belong to a coven of women I've no right touching. A fact your expression tells me you very well knew."

"Nothing has changed." She creeped toward her discarded clothes, moonlight peeking through the curtains and dancing across her skin as she moved. "I wanted one night, you gave me a night, and nothing else need ever come of it."

He took a menacing step toward her, and she matched it with a hasty step back. Temptation to shake her until she confessed, to rip the mask from her face and destroy whatever protection it gave, taunted him. But no matter what he did, it was far too late to go back. There was no taking back what they'd done.

He'd ruined her, and now he'd pay the price for indiscretion.

"Tell me your name!" It wasn't often he yelled at women, he could count the times on one hand with fingers to spare, but she'd pushed him beyond reason. For a second, she faltered, the sheet clutched so tightly her knuckles turned white, but her footing was quickly regained, and she tilted her chin up as she straightened her shoulders.

"My name is of no consequence. We haven't been introduced, and we won't *be* introduced." She bent to snatch her dress from the floor, not bothering with her corset before tugging the white satin over her head and abandoning the sheet. "This night stays here, Lord Claireborne. You will never see me again."

Another step toward her, and then another, stalking her across the room, matching every one of her backward steps until she was against the wall. Breaths coming in short puffs, her entire body rising and falling with the effort. Cheeks dusted with the glow of a satisfied woman, tormenting him with the blatant reminder of the innocence he'd stolen.

Bracing his hands on either side of her head, he captured her lips in a kiss that was far more about his anger than her pleasure. He demanded entrance, plunging and sweeping through, subduing her poor attempts to seize control. The act quickly backfired, her meager attempts to beat him at his own game drawing him deeper. Perhaps she *was* winning.

Because he was lost.

In her taste, her boldness and inexperience. In tumbling blonde curls, and luscious scarlet lips. In the body once more pressed so firmly against his, her breasts pushing into him, and in his cock coming to life once again.

Tearing his lips from hers, he stared down hard at her wide eyes and swollen lips. A rare and beautiful bloom, and still impossible to resist.

Every decision he'd made that night led to where they stood. Attending that party hadn't been in his plans until Tristan cornered him at Whites. On his way out he'd caught sight of her, intent on melting into the wall. After discovering her innocence, he proceeded to defile her for his own pleasure in the guise of giving her sexual freedom.

Now they faced the consequences of their choices, and she was scurrying like the timid little kitten she was. He couldn't allow her to vanish, there'd been far too many fatal mistakes that evening, and he refused to make another.

Whether they liked it or not, they were bound.

"What will stop me from following you home and telling your guardian exactly what you've done?"

A forced laugh crossed her lips, and she ducked beneath his arm, nearly knocking over one of Tristan's amphoras in her haste to get away. "You've no more desire to wed than I do, and I promise you if I am forced it won't be to a man like you."

"A man like me?" He raised a brow as he stalked her, inching closer as she stopped to retrieve the last of her costume. A steadying hand landed against the vase, stilling its precarious wobble. Shattering porcelain would have the entire house on them in an instant. "You certainly had no complaints about my company a few moments ago."

"You were in your element, doing exactly what it is you love to do." She offered a sly smile, the sex kitten making her appearance as she slipped her feet back into the Egyptian sandals. "And that was exactly what I needed. But dawn will break soon, and I need to return to the life I've been given. Unlike you, I'm not free to *pursue my own pleasure* by light of day."

Her fall from grace was entirely his doing, and he'd be damned if her foolish and naive confidence prevented him from doing what honor demanded. Reaching for the silk ties of her mask, permission be damned, he braced himself for the impact of revealing her identity.

"Touch it, and I'll tell Tristan you've unmasked me against my will. One more step, and I'll scream loud enough no one will hesitate to open the door." She tilted her chin, though he could swear there was the slightest tremble in it. "I may not have much power, but I have power enough."

The prospect of leading to her ruin, more than he already had, froze him in place. Defeated, he dropped his hand, breaths leaving him in sharp gusts as he stared her down.

If he pressed and she made a scene, they'd have Tristan and half the house in that room before he could blink. Then she'd be well and truly ruined, and nothing he could do would save her. Allowing her temporary freedom was the only way to protect her. "I'll thoroughly enjoy bringing you to heel."

A half smile tilted her lips as she unlocked the door. "Finding an heiress in a sea of them is quite the task. I do hope you grow to enjoy balls and the crush that comes with them. You'll need some satisfaction to temper the disappointment."

As the door closed behind her, he took several cleansing breaths. As safe as his little heiress felt behind her mask, she'd revealed far more than she realized. Luscious blonde curls, and enticingly full lips weren't reserved for the vixen, as much as he'd like to say they were.

But the interesting combination of green and gold in her eyes, and her delicate perfume, the unusual violet scent, would set her apart from most of the other debutantes. As would her familiarity with their host. Tristan had only three sisters, and he needn't look any further than their intimate circle.

His little flower was as good as found.

Afterword

Thank you so much for reading, and I do hope you enjoyed Kitty and Sebastian's entrance. Their story is far from over, and they'll soon get their happily ever after – though not quite so easily as Seb thinks. While you wait, please enjoy a preview of the two other books currently in the Innocence Lost series.

Preview of Scorned Innocence

Every woman had her limit, and Emma, youngest sister to the overbearing Duke of Westbury, teetered dangerously close to reaching hers.

She slipped into the music room and pressed her back to the door, exhaling the little air she had available. When it clicked shut, the stony facade came crashing down. There was nowhere to hide where gossip and humiliation didn't cling to her skirts, but the music room was private enough to settle her heart and hands, before someone caught her trembling.

To be shunned was one thing, to let anyone see it affect her was quite another.

Attending her first ball after a broken engagement was more daunting than she'd anticipated, and holding her head high was harder with each foray into society. Her shoulders ached under the pressure, the cramp in her neck refused to abate, and laudanum failed to ease the pain.

There was no true escape that evening, for social derision finally followed her into her own home.

She took another calming breath, and shook out the unrelenting tension in her hands, as she approached the pianoforte. Music provided solace when the world pressed too hard, offered a reprieve from reality, and sanctuary when there was nowhere else to hide. Across the smooth, cool wood, her fingers loosened up enough to dabble at a few keys before taking her seat on the bench.

The first chord came easily, then the second, and third, until she was completely lost in them. With every deep, solemn note, the humiliation, the fury, and the scandal she'd been left to face, poured from her fingers.

"You always did find the perfect song to play."

Her breath hinged on a familiar set of eyes, glittering from the shadows, his voice stealing the air from her chest, just as he'd stolen her heart all those years ago.

And crushed it.

"*Zachary.*" The warmth curling around her frosty heart was as unwelcome as he and the barnacles he'd no doubt tracked throughout her home. As his smile widened, she pinned him with a glare. "How long have you been standing there?"

The slow, insulting pull on his watch chain sent her into a fiery rage, but it never took long for that handsome smirk and flippant demeanor to douse the flames she consumed herself with. "Forty-three minutes."

"I believe the party is taking place in the ballroom. Are you incapable of navigating the halls alone, *Captain*?"

"It seems I must be. Perhaps you could escort me back?" Arrogant superiority wove through the very essence of his being, but his slow approach and devastating smile threatened to crack her resolve. "You could even join me in a dance, if you felt so compelled."

"I was unaware you'd even washed back up on shore, let alone been invited. Must have been an oversight on my mother's part. I'll make a note to discuss that with her tomorrow over tea." She forced her focus into a lilting melody, determined to ignore his presence as deftly as she could muster. "For a spare, and a pirate, you're quite forward."

The barb brought a chuckle that rippled through her, settling directly between her thighs. "Haven't you heard? Daniel snapped his neck in a race. I'm a spare no longer."

His remorse was sadly lacking, but morality and empathy had never been two of his strongest suits. His older brother had always been a fool who raced too frequently, and he'd likely wagered away half their wealth in the handful of years he'd headed the Blackmour estate.

"My brothers did mention some daft gambler losing his head. I didn't realize they meant it literally." She settled her fingers back over the keys, her toes on the pedals and posture impeccable. "I do hope he left a few pennies in your coffers."

"He may have left one or two." He stalked into the moonlight dripping in through the windows, no longer blending into his inky surroundings.

There was never a time when the way his sandy hair fell across his brow didn't soften her bitterness toward the world. Nor was there ever a moment his sapphire eyes failed to melt away the disdain she so easily fell into. Especially under the cover of darkness.

She'd once fancied herself in love with those eyes, now aged with years at sea she knew nothing about.

"Why are you hiding all the way in here, Lord Blackmour?"

"Seeking the same reprieve as you, little one." He stalked around the pianoforte, his fingers delicately caressing the sleek mahogany finish as he crept closer. Every step dragged the air from her chest, his strut so confident and erotic, she lost any reasonable thoughts.

Like how offended she should have been at the childish nickname he'd bestowed upon her so many years ago.

"I'm much more curious why *you* felt the need to seek solitude. The Emma Hemings I knew lived for these routs." He was only a meter away when he finally stopped and relaxed against the side of the piano, his unwavering attention heavier than the social weight outside that door. "You escaped a fortune hunting bastard."

She slammed the wrong key and bit her tongue until the metallic tang of blood coated it.

How *dare* he.

How dare he mention it.

How dare he smile.

How dare he even have knowledge of such compromising and personal information.

"I don't wish to speak of it. Least of all with you." She squared her shoulders, slamming harder and louder on the keys to drown out the conversation.

Every purposeful slip out of tune deepened his scowl, and he crossed his arms over his broad chest as he drifted closer. "Surely you aren't still upset about our kiss?"

She lifted her fingers and snapped her eyes to his, but every harsh word died when she found his face a breath from hers. No one had been that close to her since he said goodbye, *kissed* her goodbye, before leaving her behind to seek his destiny at sea. "What are you doing?"

"Indulging in madness." A half smile curled his lips, and her heart caught as the lines around his eyes deepened. "What would you say if I asked you to run away with me?"

Nothing but contempt from him every moment of her life, and yet he stood there, offering for her as naturally as spring brought rain. She huffed a humorless laugh, turning back to the piano, and hit another offkey note before drifting into another song. "Hunt for *your* fortune elsewhere."

"You were never meant for simpering and unfaithful men, for dinner parties and empty conversation. I see the fire in your eyes." He stalked to the other side of the piano, securing their positions as predator and prey. "You're too good for London, Emma."

It'd be a cold day in hell before she allowed her childhood antagonist to talk her into more torment by whisking her away to sea.

Alone.

With no one to help her if he so chose to leave her on some primitive Caribbean Island.

He had to have been driven mad on that little boat of his, because that could be the only driving force behind the unprovoked proposition. "I won't be your fool again."

He slowly maneuvered around the piano, stealing her breath with each step. When he slipped from her peripheral vision, her entire body went rigid, her mind racing with all sorts of imaginings. Scoundrels did all manner of things in the shadows when no one was watching.

Delicately she played, as his hot breath fanned the back of her neck, his hair tickling her ear. A light pressure settled over her waist as he rested his hands over her stays, and she struggled to keep her breaths even.

"That would imply you were a fool then."

He pressed his mouth to the curve of her neck, and her eyes slipped closed at the heated contact. She'd been kissed before, there, but it'd never tickled like a thousand tiny fires dancing along her skin, or filled her body with so much heat, settling between her thighs.

Like a molten pool bubbling to life deep in her pelvis. It was sorcery, a wicked deception from a demon sent straight from the bowels of hell. She needed to break free, get away from him, before he dragged her down to Hades and never let her escape.

"Zach, don't." She whirled from him, willing her stampeding heart to calm as she backed away, every step weighing her down with fear and regret. Fear she might enjoy the attention he meant to lavish upon her, and regret she was pushing away the only man she'd ever wanted.

The only man who made her feel alive.

Accepted.

Worthy.

"Coward." He'd accused her of that exact thing, before hopping on a ship and leaving her behind, and it never failed to hit its mark.

"Excuse me?"

An infuriating chuckle emanated from deep in his chest as he removed his hands, cold settling in their wake. A loss she didn't want to feel with him. "You heard me."

"I won't let you take advantage again."

"Oh, little one." He stepped closer, sliding his hand through her hair, reaching up to cup her cheek.

Time hinged on her breaths, and the clock stopped ticking. A terrifying sincerity reflected in his eyes, but she'd be a fool to believe in it again. The blow to her ego was too fresh for her to indulge in his return, but neither could she pull away.

He ran his thumb across her jaw, eyes following down the length of her neck. "No one could ever take advantage of you."

Preview of Surrendered Innocence

There was nothing Isla could do to save her savage rogue.

Her father conspired that very moment with Lord Eberlin to capture Caden, ensure his hanging, and collect the staggering reward on his head. All she could do was pray he got out of London alive.

That he'd run as fast and as far as he could.

That she'd never see him again, despite her own suffering.

The bed ceased calling to her hours ago, the window and its entrancing oblivion beckoned instead. It was impossible to find peace when Caden was out in that storm. Even Mother Nature conspired against them, exposing him to the winter elements. The sleet pelting the bedroom window muffled her slippered footsteps, and the darkness beyond reached inside her chamber, inviting her to abandon all sense.

Her heart and soul screamed to run away from London, and everything keeping them apart. Duty and honor shackled her since birth; her place was in England, married to Lord Eberlin.

So the world said.

Being Lady Isla Hawthorne was a terribly heavy weight to shoulder, and she was far too close to crumbling under the pressure. She tipped her face to the ceiling, pleading with God to spare her love's life and allow her some peace.

The onyx world beyond her window promised nothing but empti-ness, and she spun toward the bedroom door, her thick, auburn braid falling over her shoulder with the hasty escape.

There was little she could do to stave off the chill coming from within, but the movement fed her need for some purpose. She stalked toward the fire, rubbing her upper arms as she stole a glance at the mantle clock, but the time slipped from her consciousness as a harsh rattling broke through the silence. Isla froze mid step as her eyes shifted to the window.

A brawny figure filled the entirety of the pane as the urgent rattling intensified. Cold fear washed over her, chasing away logic, and she ran for her life, unwilling to wait for an identity. Heavy boots stomped across the floor, soggy soles filling her ears and foreboding unspeakable ruin.

Before she could reach the door or scream for help, a freezing hand clamped tight over her mouth and tugged her hard against an icy chest. Sopping wet and frozen to the bone. Fear tore a sharp cry from her throat, but the hand robbed it of any meaningful sound.

"Easy, Wisp." The whispered brogue caressed her ear, releasing tension from every muscle in her body.

Prying his fingers loose, she faced him, the smug grin setting a match to her fury fueled by fear. Not knowing if he was alive or dead, there or gone, safe or tormented, had frayed her nerves for hours. His dark hair clung to his forehead, droplets slipping from the tips of his hair down his face.

And he had the audacity to smile, as though he'd popped round for tea and biscuits. Every emotion welled inside her, a tidal wave that couldn't be stopped, and she closed the already miniscule distance between them. She reared back and let her hand fly, catching him across the cheek and filling the silence with a wet crack. "Don't you *dare* scare me like that again."

His smile emboldened as he rubbed the offended cheek. "But you love the chase, my little Wisp. You live for the thrill of it."

Despair replaced every other emotion, as she set herself to memorizing the feel of muscle beneath soaked linen, the way just being near him threatened to lull her into a very false sense of comfort. "You should be halfway to the border by now."

He tucked the unruly braid behind her ear, and she leaned her cheek into his palm as he withdrew his touch with a soft caress. "I must be gone well before dawn, but I cannae leave without you."

"They'll kill you if they find you."

"Which is why we must make haste. Every moment spent under this roof is a moment lost, and we've none to spare." A nervous glance to the door betrayed the lurking anxiety beneath his unaffected exterior.

"I'll slow you down, give them more reason to follow you into hell, and fuel their need to see you hung." Her heart hammered as the last regretful word slipped from her lips, and his arms curled around her, her night dress as soaked and frigid as his clothing. "You're so cold."

"Not with you in my arms." He crushed her to him, pressing his lips to the top of her head. "Let us be on our way. Find lodging, trade these clothes for dry ones."

She pressed her cheek to his chest, too afraid to look him in his eyes. Temptation taunted her, pleaded with her to obey and climb out the window at his side, but he'd never make it across the border if he brought her along.

Whether it be her father's men or the weather, his demise was assured if she indulged his whims. He needed to go, she needed to stay, and pretending any other ending was plausible only worsened his chance of escape.

Hounds bayed in the distance, and her heart seized as her knuckles went white for their ironclad grip on his shirt. "You need to go. Now." All she'd have left of him were memories, and good or bad she needed to know exactly which man had stolen her heart.

A man who committed cold blooded murder, as her father claimed him to be, or an innocent Highlander, framed for a nonexistent crime.

Lord Eberlin refused to disclose a victim's name, just claimed he'd witnessed Caden engaged in a duel. But she couldn't believe that, couldn't reconcile the accusations with the man she loved.

An overpowering need to hear the truth from his own lips consumed her as she pressed her body fully to his, hoping to transfer some of her heat, and absorb the chill from his bones. "Tell me Lord Eberlin is wrong, that you didn't kill a man in cold blood."

"That bastard just wants to see me dead, Wisp. I did *not* kill anyone." He tightened his arm around her waist and pinned her down beneath shadowed eyes, relief melting her body into his arms.

"Come with me, lass, please."

Pain sliced through her soul with a dull blade, carving the very heart from her chest. She forced her lips to move, the words out of her mouth. They were worth his life, and she'd do anything to ensure he kept it. "I could never forgive myself if I was the reason you were caught and hung. Do not ask me to plunge a dagger through your heart."

He pressed his lips gently to hers, a kiss so painfully sweet her chest ached. No man who kissed like that could be bad. Could have so coldly taken a life. "You say I cannae ask you to run a blade through my chest, but you cannae ask me to leave you to that bastard Eberlin. I cannae abide it, Isla. I *willnae* abide it."

The prospect of spending the rest of her life with Lord Eberlin, of the paunch fortune hunting opportunist being the first and only man allowed access to her body, sent a disgusted chill over her flesh. Even colder than Caden's embrace.

She'd meant to marry *him*, spend the rest of her days filling *their* home with heirs to spare. They'd raise them on the wild moors, away from that same duty and obligation that ripped them apart.

"Do you think *I* can abide him taking what's meant to be yours? Just the thought of his hands on my body..." Nausea halted the words, her grip tightening on Caden.

But, it didn't have to be that way.

It was madness, but if that night was all she could ever have, she'd gladly suffer whatever consequences the choice might bring. She nuzzled into the crook of his neck. "Let us pretend for a few moments that I'm yours, and you're mine. Let me pretend my body won't belong to another by morning."

"Pretend?" He reared back but clung to her nightdress, brows drawn over his nose. His dark green eyes slowly raked over her face and the length of her neck, burning a hole straight through her heart. The feral rumble emanating from his chest rattled and called to an intimate part of her demanding satiety at his hands. "You *are* mine, Wisp."

"I desperately wish to be, but my father has already broken us apart. Don't you see that?" Her heart thrummed, knocking the air from her lungs with each erratic and desperate throb. "You are dead or you are gone, but you are not mine and I cannot be yours."

"I dinnae care where I am, or where you are. Your body and beauty are mine, and I'll ensure you never doubt it."

Bookshelf

<u>Regency</u>

Masked Innocence

Surrendered Innocence

<u>Contemporary</u>

I've Got You

A Very Bossy Holiday

About the Author

Sawyer lives a quiet, but never boring, life in a small New England town that isn't as quaint as you'd think. And it's definitely, and regretfully, nowhere near the ocean. Instead, she spends her days dreaming of the sea and spinning wild tales about alpha heroes and the women who slay them like so many dragons.

@AuthorSawyerQuinn will track her down on most socials, but she's typically the most active on Pinterest and IG. Pinterest will also give you a glimpse into her mind, and what is percolating for stories ahead.

Sign up for her newsletter to stay in the know and receive a FREE copy of Scorned Innocence – currently, the only way to get it.

www.sawyerquinn.com